Story: Gilles Tibo
Illustrations: Philippe Germa...

Alex and the New Equipment

LITTLE WOLF BOOKS
level
3

I love books

Dominique & Friends

Canadian Cataloguing in Publication Data

Tibo, Gilles, 1951-
(Alex numéro 2. English)
Alex and the new equipment
(Little wolf books. Level 3, I love books)
Translation of: Alex numéro 2.

ISBN 1-894363-09-4

I. Germain, Philippe, 1963- II. Homel, David
III. Title. IV. Title: Alex numéro 2. English. V. Series.

PS8589.I26A8513 1999 jC843'.54 C99-900662-2
PZ7.T4333Aln 1999

Series Editor: Lucie Papineau
Art direction and design: Primeau & Barey
English version: David Homel

Legal Deposit: 3rd Quarter 1999
Bibliothèque nationale du Québec
National Library of Canada

Printed in Canada

10 9 8 7 6 5 4 3 2

Dominique & Friends
A division of Les éditions Héritage inc.

Canada:
300 Arran Street, Saint Lambert,
Quebec, Canada J4R 1K5

USA:
P.O. Box 800
Champlain, New York
12919

Tel.: 1-888-228-1498
Fax: 1-888-782-1481
E-mail: info@editionsheritage.com

The publisher wishes to thank the Canada Council for its support, as well as SODEC and Canadian Heritage.

Le Conseil des Arts du Canada depuis 1957 | The Canada Council for the Arts since 1957

SODEC
Société de développement des entreprises culturelles
Québec ::

*For Simon Ménard-Dunn,
the best right winger in the world!*

TIBO

Preface

Hi! My name is Antoine Vaillancourt Dutil. I'm ten years old. I used to play a lot of hockey. But I stopped because my equipment got too little and too worn out. I already have my list of presents for next Christmas. I wrote down, "I'd like to receive a new set of hockey equipment because I'm just as nice as Alex, the hero of thi book."

Before I forget, I want to remind you that Alex is back with more adventures—and a new sweater. Just a minute, the phone is ringing...

That's my best friend, he wants to play hockey with me! Here I go, and who cares about the equipment? As long as you have fun!

I hope you'll enjoy reading and playing, too!

Antoine Vaillancourt Dutil
Cap-Rouge, Quebec

My father, my mother, my friends and everyone who knows me call me Alex Number 1. Why? Because I'm the world's greatest hockey player. I practiced so hard that my sweater got all worn out. It's so full of holes I can't wear it any more.

My mother told me, "Don't worry, Alex, sweaters always wear out."

My father said, "I'll give you another one. I just hope you won't write *Number 1* on this one!"

I went into my room with my dog Toolie.
I took a marker and wrote "Alex Number 2"
on my sweater, because it's my second one.

Now I'm Alex Number 2.

It took a few weeks, but everyone got used to my new name. My father, my mother, my neighbours and my friends call me Alex Number 2.

I practice every day in the alley. With my Number 2 sweater, I can score a thousand goals a day.

Even though I have a new hockey sweater, it would still be great to get some real equipment, the kind real players wear. I wrote down a list of presents I'd like to receive for Christmas, or my birthday, or just because I've been nice.

"Hockey skates," I wrote, "and a hockey stick, a real hockey sweater, hockey pads, hockey gloves, a hockey helmet, a hockey rink, a hockey arena and a Stanley Cup.

"Thank you very much!"

I just can't wait any more! I need hockey equipment, right now. I dug through the kitchen cupboards, the closets, my parents' drawers, even my father's toolbox. And I found everything, everything I needed!

I went into my room with my dog Toolie. I taped a note on the door:

DO NOT ENTER! PLAYERS' DRESSING ROOM!

I started to make myself some new equipment. For my helmet, I put a salad bowl on my head, then tied it on with a shoelace. To test how solid it was, I hit my noggin a few times on the chest of drawers. It worked great! I didn't even have a headache.

Next, I slipped some plastic food containers under my sweater, then ran into the wall a few times. Excellent! As good as real shoulder pads!

I put on my father's great big socks,
and stuffed them with newspapers.
I banged my stick against my legs,
and didn't feel any pain at all.
Magnificent! Just like real shin
guards!

Then I took my mother's high-heeled shoes.
With some laces, I tied metal files underneath.
A masterpiece! As good as real skates!

For the finishing touch, I put on my father's big
mittens. Then I looked in the mirror. YAHOO!
Finally I looked like a real hockey player. This
was the best day of my life!

I started playing in my room with my new equipment. I really was the best player in the world. Toolie did his best to try and stop the ball, but today, my shot was as good as the top scorer's in the National Hockey League. My slapshots were as fast and hard as a hailstorm.

I ran, I jumped on the bed, between the chairs, on the chest of drawers. The ball bounced off the floor, the walls, even the ceiling. Suddenly, CRACK! The ball broke my window.

My mother came running into the hallway and opened my door. Her hair stood up straight on her head. She caught me standing on the furniture. My room was upside down. There was a big hole in the window.

To make her laugh, I said, "There are still two minutes left in overtime."

It was no time for jokes. I lowered my head and said, "I'm sorry. I'll put back all the stuff I borrowed. I'll clean up my room and help pay for the new window by... by... by opening a juice stand."

The next morning, I woke up early. My parents were still sleeping. I went down to the kitchen and opened the fridge door. I took out two jugs of juice and a stack of plastic cups. I set it all out on the sidewalk in front of our house, on a table.

On a piece of cardboard, I wrote,

FRESH ORANGE JUICE
50¢ A GLASS
(TO PAY FOR THE
WINDOW I BROKE)

All the neighbours bought juice from me. Some people were thirstier than others. They bought two glasses. Scott Lawrence, on his way back from jogging, asked for three.

My father showed up in his bathrobe, his hair all in a mess. I handed him the money and said,

FRESH ORANGE Juice
50¢ A GLASS
(TO PAY FOR TH
WINDOW I BROK

"Here, now the window is paid for."

He slipped the money into his pocket. He yawned and stretched.

"I wouldn't mind drinking something, too."

"Sorry, there's none left!"

Suddenly I got a great idea. I borrowed some money from my father. I ran down to the grocery store and bought all the juice I could pay for. Then I came back with my arms full. I served my father a big glass, and gave one to my mother, who was just getting up.

Then I went outside to my table again. On another piece of cardboard, I wrote,

FRESH ORANGE JUICE
50¢ A GLASS
(TO BUY EQUIPMENT
FOR THE BEST
HOCKEY PLAYER IN
THE WORLD)

To sell my wares, I called out,

I'll get my new equipment, sooner or later, even if I have to sell orange juice all summer—and ice cream cones all winter!

End of the second period.